Dear mouse friends,
Welcome to the world of

Geronimo Stilton

The Editorial Staff of
The Rodent's Gazette

1. Linda Thinslice
2. Sweetie Cheesetriangle
3. Ratella Redfur
4. Soya Mousehao
5. Cheesita de la Pampa
6. Coco Chocamouse
7. Mouseanna Mousetti
8. Patty Plumprat
9. Tina Spicytail
10. William Shortpaws
11. Valerie Vole
12. Trap Stilton
13. Dolly Fastpaws
14. Zeppola Zap
15. Merenguita Gingermouse
16. Shorty Tao
17. Baby Tao
18. Gigi Gogo
19. Teddy von Muffler
20. Thea Stilton
21. Erronea Misprint
22. Pinky Pick
23. Ya-ya O'Cheddar
24. Ratsy O'Shea
25. Geronimo Stilton
26. Benjamin Stilton
27. Briette Finerat
28. Raclette Finerat
29. Mousella MacMouser
30. Kreamy O'Cheddar
31. Blasco Tabasco
32. Toffie Sugarsweet
33. Tylerat Truemouse
34. Larry Keys
35. Michael Mouse

Geronimo Stilton
A learned and brainy
mouse; editor of
The Rodent's Gazette

Thea Stilton
Geronimo's sister and
special correspondent at
The Rodent's Gazette

Trap Stilton
An awful joker;
Geronimo's cousin and
owner of the store
Cheap Junk for Less

Benjamin Stilton
A sweet and loving
nine-year-old mouse;
Geronimo's favorite
nephew

Geronimo Stilton

THE WILD, WILD WEST

Scholastic Inc.

New York   Toronto   London   Auckland   Sydney

Mexico City   New Delhi   Hong Kong   Buenos Aires

ISBN 978-0-439-69144-4

Copyright © 2005 by Edizioni Piemme S.p.A., Via Tiziano 32, 20145 Milan, Italy.

International Rights © Atlantyca S.p.A.

English translation © 2005 by Edizioni Piemme S.p.A.

Based on an original idea by Elisabetta Dami.

www.geronimostilton.com

Published by Scholastic Inc., 557 Broadway, New York, NY 10012. SCHOLASTIC and associated logos are trademarks and/or registered trademarks of Scholastic Inc.

Text by Geronimo Stilton
Original title *Quattro topi nel far west!*
Cover by Giuseppe Ferrario
Illustrations by Larry Keys and Ratterto Rattonchi
Graphics by Merenguita Gingermouse and Zeppola Zap

Special thanks to Kathryn Cristaldi
Interior design by Kay Petronio

26

13 14 15 16/0

Printed in the U.S.A.
First printing, July 2005

40

THEY SAY I'M A SCAREDY MOUSE

Do you know me? My name is Stilton, *Geronimo Stilton*.

I am the editor of the most POPULAR paper in New Mouse City. It's called *The Rodent's Gazette*. Most mice would agree, I'm a *pretty brainy rodent*. And I absolutely LOVE to read.

Geronimo Stilton!

After a hard day at the office,
I like to relax in my cozy mouse hole.
I slip into my fluffy cat-fur slippers.
Then I settle down with a good book
in front of the fireplace.
I make myself a nice cup of hot cheddar tea. Yum!
And sometimes I put on some soft music.

Of course, some rodents might say I am a little on the boring side. Like my sister Thea and my cousin Trap. They make fun of

Ah, what a perfect way to escape from the rat race

me because I **DON'T** like to travel. They say I'm a **SCAREDY MOUSE**. You see, I am not the adventurous type. But that is because...

...*I GET SEASICK*

...Heights make me dizzy

...and I'm a worrywart

Now, you are probably wondering what I am doing in this adventure. It takes place in the wild, **WILD WEST**. Out West you will find sun-scorched deserts, raging bulls, and even poisonous snakes.

Why would I, Geronimo "Scaredy Mouse" Stilton, travel to a place like that?

Read this book and you'll understand....

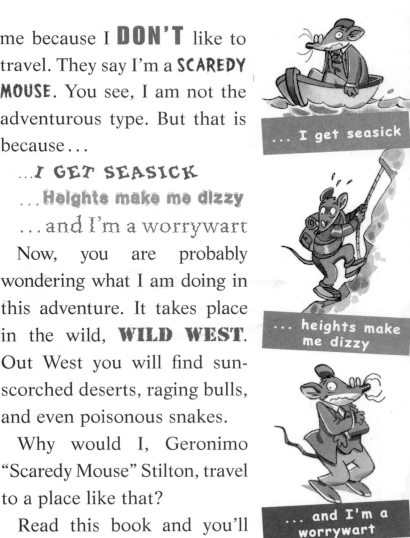

... I get seasick

... heights make me dizzy

... and I'm a worrywart

THE WILD WEST AND THE NATIVE AMERICANS

The term Wild West began to be used in the 1800s to describe the regions of the Great Plains and the Rocky Mountains, which extend west of the Mississippi River to the coast of the Pacific Ocean. Native Americans, formerly called Indians, inhabited these immense territories.

These peoples, also called redskins for their custom of smearing red earth over their entire bodies, were made up of many tribes. Here are the better-known ones:

APACHE: Brave warriors who were feared for their raids on settlers for food and livestock. Two chiefs became legendary: Cochise and Geronimo.

BLACKFEET: Able shoemakers, the Blackfeet people made moccasins of dark skins — that's how they got their name. They used dogs instead of horses to carry loads.

CHEROKEE: The Cherokee were devoted to hunting as well as farming. Around 1820, Chief Sequoya invented an alphabet made up of eighty-five symbols in order to better communicate with white people.

CHEYENNE: The Cheyenne people traveled around the plains, living in tepees. These tents were made of animal skins and formed a cone that was easy to pack and carry. The Cheyenne fought side by side with the great chiefs of the Sioux tribe in the struggle to free the Indian people.

COMANCHE: Famous for their horse-riding ability, the Comanche fought to defend their territory from white hunters who killed the buffalo and other wildlife.

SIOUX: This tribe of the Great Plains was subdivided into three groups: the Dakota, the Nakota, and the Lakota. Famous chiefs of the Sioux included Sitting Bull, Crazy Horse, and Red Cloud.

FOUR MICE IN THE WILD WEST

It was HOT.

It was dry.

It was a bad, bad fur day. Even my tail was sweating.

Oh, what I wouldn't give for a cold CHEDDAR ICE POP from my mega-huge fridge. Too bad I couldn't get one. Do you want to know why?

Because I was in the Arizona desert.

Yes, mouse fans, I, Geronimo Stilton, was in the

Lucky for me, I wasn't alone. My sister Thea, my cousin Trap, and my little nephew Benjamin were with me. Together we were crossing the scorching desert.

Have you ever been to a desert? There is not much to see. Just **SAND**, rocks, and cacti.

The sand burned my paws. I kept tripping over the rocks. And my tail was getting ripped to shreds on all those pointy cactus needles. *YOUCH!*

Worst of all, I was dying of thirst. I shook my canteen. It was **EMPTY**.

Just then a dark shadow fell over me. I gulped. Something told me it wasn't Santa Mouse flying by on his way to his summer place. I looked up.

Rancid rat hairs! It was a hungry pack of **VULTURES** waiting to lick our bones.

This place was a total **NIGHTMARE**!

WELCOME TO CACTUS CITY!

After a billion years, we finally reached a dusty set of railroad tracks.

Cheesecake! We were saved! The tracks led us to a wooden sign. In big letters it read:

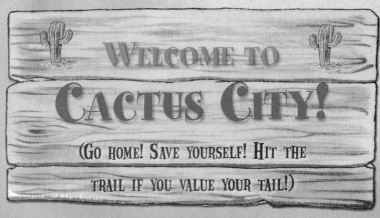

WELCOME TO

CACTUS CITY!

(GO HOME! SAVE YOURSELF! HIT THE

TRAIL IF YOU VALUE YOUR TAIL!)

I twisted my tail up in knots. "Uh-oh," I gulped. "This doesn't look **GOOD**. This doesn't look **GOOD** at all. In fact, this looks **DOWNRIGHT BAD**, if you ask me."

Trap pushed me forward. "Oh, don't be such a scaredy mouse, Germeister," he snorted. He gave me another shove.

I tumbled headfirst into a cactus. "Don't push me! I can't stand it when you push me!" I yelled, picking **NEEDLES** out of my fur.

Have I told you my cousin Trap is the most **ANNOYING** rodent on the planet?

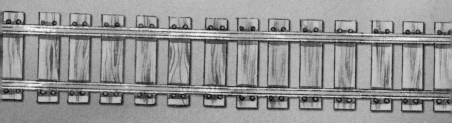

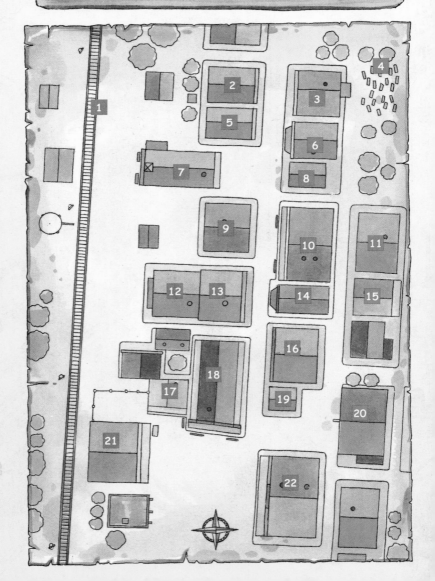

MAP OF CACTUS CITY

1 Railroad

2 Lawyer

3 Undertaker

4 Cemetery

5 Courthouse

6 Dress Shop

7 Barn

8 Blacksmith

9 General Store

10 Saloon

11 School

12 Railroad Station

13 Depot

14 Printer

15 Schoolteacher's House

16 Sheriff

17 Trading Post

18 Bank

19 Jail

20 Doctor's House

21 Hotel

22 Infirmary

THE LAW IN THE WILD WEST

At first, no one was concerned with public order in the towns of the Wild West. Then the government of the United States sent sheriffs and judges to keep order and to enforce the law.

WHAT'S WRONG WITH CACTUS CITY?

A wiry old mouse stood in front of the railroad station. He was dressed in a uniform.

"**Howdy**, strangers, what brings you to Cactus City?" he called, waving us over. "The name's Choo-Choo Cheddar, that's C.C. for short," he chattered. "I lend a paw down here at the **station**. Yep, been working here for some twenty years. I sell tickets, carry bags. Yep, you name it, I've done it. Sometimes I even..."

Suddenly C.C. stopped in mid-sentence. I noticed he was staring at us with an **odd** expression on his snout.

"Well, **GOLLY**," he cried. "You mouselings must have come from way far off yonder. Just look at your duds. Shucks, you're dressed just like city mice."

C.C. offered us some stewed beans and a sip of water.

"Sorry I can't get you more to drink," he said in a low voice. "Water is hard to come by in these parts." He looked around nervously. Then he whispered, "Let me give you some advice, strangers. Get out of town now!"

How strange. What was wrong with Cactus City? It looked like a nice little town to me.

I was still thinking about C.C.'s words

Choo-Choo Cheddar the Stationmaster

CURLY THE TRAIN CONDUCTOR

when a train rumbled into the station.

A rat with long, waxed whiskers got off. It was Curly *THE TRAIN CONDUCTOR*.

"Cactus City! Last station before the desert!" he yelled.

No one got off the train. No one stopped in **Cactus City**.

How strange. What was wrong with Cactus City?

We decided to check out the town.

First we passed the **BLACKSMITH'S** shop. A huge musclemouse was hammering

BUCK THE BLACKSMITH

Doc Squeakers

away on a piece of metal. He was making a horseshoe.

A mouse carrying a *doctor's* bag scampered by. "Clear the way!" he squeaked. "Nancy Nibbler's about to have those triplets!"

A plump mouse stuck his head out a building door. It was the **banker**. He looked around nervously. Then he raced back inside.

I wondered why he looked so worried.

Just then I heard a familiar noise. It was a `printing press`!

Rex the Banker

Tommy the Printer

A rat with tiny glasses was busy printing the newspaper. He glanced up at us suspiciously.

We passed by a courthouse. An old *judge* peeked out the door. He looked around. Then he slammed the door shut.

In front of the saloon, a rodent sat in a ROCKING CHAIR. A big hat covered his face. He stopped rocking when we walked by. How odd. I thought he was napping. But it seemed as if he was hiding from something.

Minutes later, we ran into the UNDERTAKER. He shook our paws warmly.

He had a huge grin plastered on his face. *At least one rodent wasn't worried*, I thought. "Welcome to Cactus City, strangers!" The undertaker beamed. "If I can be of service, don't be shy. Today I'm having a two-for-one special. Yessiree, that's two stiffs for the price of one!"

A bucktoothed rodent stood next to him. He held up a shovel. I guess he was a gravedigger. "Just tell me how deep and I'll dig it!"

I shivered. Then I noticed something else that was strange about Cactus City.

There was no SHERIFF. Do you know what a sheriff does? He keeps order in the town. He locks up bad rodents in his jail. Sort of like the Chief of Police in New Mouse City.

BORIS THE UNDERTAKER AND GRIMSLY THE GRAVEDIGGER

IF MY FRIENDS COULD SEE ME NOW

We found the general store in the center of town. Inside, a short, stocky mouse greeted us.

"Howdy, strangers! Welcome to **BLUNT RAT BOB'S**!" he squeaked. "Bob's the name. Stuff is my game. And, strangers, do you look like you need some stuff! Those duds you're wearing look **ridiculous**!"

BOB THE GENERAL STORE OWNER

I stared down at my suit. I guess I did look out of place. But ridiculous? No way.

Meanwhile, Bob had run off. He returned a few minutes later with a pawful of **CLOTHES**.

I pulled on a pair of leather pants, boots with spurs, a checkered shirt, and a cowrat hat. Then I looked at myself in the mirror. I must admit, I looked pretty cool. I felt just like a real **COWRAT**. "If only my friends at *The Rodent's Gazette* could see me now."

My family seemed just as excited.

Benjamin jumped up and down. "If only my friends at school could see me now!" he exclaimed.

Trap wiggled his tail. "If only my friends down at the Squeak and Chew could see me now," he chuckled.

Thea winked at her own reflection. Then she tried to take a step. She tried to jump. She tried to run. But her *dress* was so long she couldn't move. Instead, she fell *flat* on her snout!

"Thank goodness my friends can't see me

now," she snorted. She had Bob bring her a pair of pants, a shirt, and a pretty bandanna.

"That's better," she nodded. "Now all I need is a **HORSE** and I'm ready for **ACTION**!"

Bob pointed to four horses in front of his store.

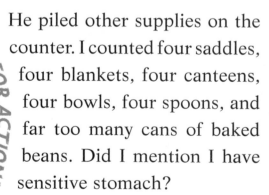

He piled other supplies on the counter. I counted four saddles, four blankets, four canteens, four bowls, four spoons, and far too many cans of baked beans. Did I mention I have sensitive stomach?

MY COUSIN WILL PAY!

"That's what you need, strangers," Bob said when he had gathered all our supplies. "Now, how will you be paying?"

Trap pointed to me. "My cousin will pay!" he squeaked.

I wasn't surprised. Trap loves spending money...especially when it's mine.

I pulled out some bills from my wallet. Bob eyed them with **SUSPICION**.

"Never saw bills like this," he said. "Nope, you need gold in these parts, stranger."

With a sigh, I gave him my **GOLD** watch.

gold watch

"Not enough, partner," he said, pocketing the watch. "I'll need more GOLD. What else do you have?"

gold tooth

Before I could think, Trap spoke up. "My cousin has a GOLD tooth," he announced.

Bob took out a pair of pliers. "Open up," he ordered.

Cheese nibblets! He was going to yank out my GOLD tooth! I felt faint.

Just then, my sister jumped to my rescue. "Stop! Don't touch him!" she shrieked. "I've got lots of GOLD for you." Good old Thea.

I watched as she plunked down all of her GOLD jewelry on the counter.

"Not enough!" Bob declared.

At that moment, Trap mumbled something under his breath. Then he pulled

gold jewelry

out a GOLD chain that was hidden under his shirt. On it hung a giant shiny GOLD letter *T*.

gold chain

We all stared at it. That *T* must have weighed a ton.

Still Bob insisted it wasn't enough.

I was getting **ANNOYED**. What more did this mouse want from us? Our firstborn mouselings?

It was time to put my paw down. Our GOLD was worth at least a few scruffy-looking horses. But before I could squeak, Benjamin **PIPED UP**.

"Mr. Bob, I don't have any GOLD," he began. "But maybe you'd like my new Cheese Blaster 4000 game."

He pulled a small electronic video game from his backpack. Colorful pictures of Swiss slices and mozzarella balls zoomed

video game

across the screen.

Bob's eyes LIT UP like my grandfather Cheap Mouse Willy's when he discovers a penny on the sidewalk.

"You've got a deal!" he squeaked. "This toy is fabumouse!"

By now, it was already dusk. We gathered our supplies and took off.

We needed to find a place to spend the night. *BUT WHERE*? Where do you spend the night in the **wild, wild west?** Something told me there were no Five-star Furtown Hotels in Cactus City.

"DEAL!"

SQUEAKYTIME TEA?

Just then we spotted a sign tacked to the front of the saloon. It read:

ROOMS FOR RENT!

Thea clapped her paws. "Okay, everyone. Here's what we're going to do," she announced. "Gerry Berry will go into the saloon. He will book us two rooms for the night. The rest of us will take care of the horses."

One thing you should know about Thea—she loves being the boss.

I stared at the noisy saloon. "Can't you come in with me?" I asked. I'm a little shy in front of strangers.

Trap pushed me toward the door. "Oh, stop being

"GO ON, 'FRAIDY MOUSE!"

such a 'FRAIDY MOUSE!" he snorted. "Shake a paw!"

I frowned. "Don't *push* me! I can't stand it when you push me!" I squeaked.

I stepped into the saloon. Cowrats were everywhere. They were playing cards. They were flinging darts. They were picking their teeth with pocketknives. *Rat-munching rattlesnakes!* Those cowrats were tough!

I listened to one rodent banging away at the piano. He was awful. But I didn't dare say a word. He might use *me* to pick his teeth!

Just then a mouse **screeched** at me from behind the bar.

"What d'ya want, stranger?" he yelled. My stomach was churning. I guess it was the beans.

I decided a hot cup of **Squeakytime**

Tea would be just perfect. So I asked him for one.

His mouth hit the floor. "Did you say a hot cup of **Squeakytime Tea**?" he repeated.

I nodded. I wondered why he looked so surprised. I know the name sounds silly, but it really is a very *soothing* tea.

He snorted and turned to the crowd. "Did ya hear what the stranger wants to drink?" he bellowed. "**Squeakytime Tea**!"

The piano player stopped playing.

Everyone turned toward me. They were quiet as mice.

Then they started laughing. "**Squeakytime Tea?** Ha-ha-haaa!!"

The bartender slid a cup of tea down the counter toward me . . . but I missed.

The bartender threw
me a cup of tea...

then a second cup of tea...

...and a third... This time
I caught it on the fly!

The crowd snickered.

The bartender threw me
a second cup of tea... but
I missed again.

They all guffawed.

The bartender threw me
a third cup.

This time
I caught it
on the fly.

It was my turn to sneer.
So I did. Then I let out an
ear-piercing scream.

The cup was scalding
hot!

STRANGER, CACTUS CITY IS TOO SMALL FOR THE TWO OF US!

I blew on my paws. They felt like they were on fire.

I started hopping around in a circle screaming, "*OUCH, OUCH, OUCH!*"

Then I heard a crunch. Oops! I had accidentally stepped on someone's paw.

I turned around. I was snout to snout with an ugly rat with **HUMONGOUS MUSCLES**. Yikes!

"S-s-s-soorry," I stammered.

He gnashed his teeth. "You did that on purpose!"

OUCH!

he **ROARED**. Then he spit into a **METAL BUCKET** across the room. *Ping!* Perfect shot.

I turned pale. "No, really, it was an accident," I tried to explain.

He didn't let me finish. "Stranger, **Cactus City** is too small for the two of us!" he declared.

It was an accident!

MICK MUSCLE MOUSE

I was shivering in my boots. Oh, why did I have to step on this cowrat's toes? He was bigger than a pro rat wrestler.

"Of course, I'll leave immediately," I muttered.

But the rodent held up his paw. "Too *late*, stranger," he squeaked. "No one messes with Mick Muscle Mouse and gets away with it. We need to fight it out. One of us will live, and the other will be *PUSHING UP DAISIES*."

The UNDERTAKER applauded. "Pushing up daisies. I like it!" He leaned out the door and yelled to the gravedigger. "Hey, Grimsly, get a *casket* ready!" he instructed. "On second thought, make that two *caskets*. We might get lucky!"

Then he looked me up and down. "So, stranger, what's your name?" he asked.

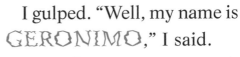

BORIS RATINSKY & CO. FUNERAL PARLOR

I gulped. "Well, my name is GERONIMO," I said.

G as in **GENTLE**.

E as in **EDUCATED**.

R as in **RESPECTFUL**.

O as in **OH, I AM SO SORRY THAT I STEPPED ON MICK MUSCLE MOUSE'S PAW!**

N as in **NOT DONE ON PURPOSE**.

I as in **I AM A POLITE MOUSE**.

M as in **MY, OH, MY, HOW DID I EVER GET INTO THIS MESS?**

O as in **OH, POOR, POOR ME!**

The undertaker chiseled my name on the coffin. "Uhm, let's see, that's *GERONIMO*..."

G as in **GONNA PAY ME IN ADVANCE WHILE YOU'RE STILL BREATHING.**

E as in **EVERYBODY HAS TO KICK THE BUCKET SOONER OR LATER.**

R as in you **REALLY BLEW IT THIS TIME.**

O as in **OH, WHY DID YOU STOP IN CACTUS CITY?**

N as in **NO ONE LASTS LONG HERE.**

I as in **I PITY YOU....**

M as in **MAYBE YOU'LL TELL ME WHY YOU STEPPED ON THE FOOT OF MICK MUSCLE MOUSE, OF ALL RODENTS?**

O as in **OH, WELL, HOPE YOU HAD A NICE LIFE!**

Mick jumped to his paws. "Let me at him!" he shrieked. "I'll flatten him! I'll mash him into cottage cheese! I'll skin him like a rat-fur rug! I'll spread him out like cream cheese!"

YOO-HOO!

At that moment, a voice **sang out**. "Yoo-hoo! Mick Muscle Mouse! How are you doing this morning?" it trilled.

A pretty blonde rodent with bright blue eyes stood in front of us. She was dressed all in pink from her snout to her tail. In her paw she carried a pink umbrella.

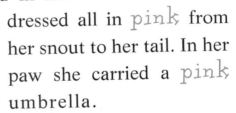

It was Miss Dolly Dandywhiskers. She owned the Pretty Paws Dress Shop in town.

"Why, Miss Dolly," Mick gushed. "You're looking lovely today."

Miss Dolly, the proprietress of the dress shop

It was then that I noticed Mick's fur had turned beet-red. Was he coming down with something? Rodent pox? The flu? A terrible case of sunburn? Then I realized he was beaming at Miss Dolly. I snickered. Yep, Mick Muscle Mouse was sick all right. He was LOVESICK!

Just then, Dolly dropped her tiny lace handkerchief on the ground.

Mick let go of my ear. He ran to pick up Dolly's handkerchief.

Dolly smiled. *"Oh, thank you so much, Mr. Muscle Mouse,"* she gushed.

Mick grinned. I grinned, too. Not because those two were in love. But because Mick had completely forgotten about me!

I GRABBED MY TAIL AND RAN!

SAVED BY A WHISKER!

I searched all over for my family. But it was as if they had disappeared.

They were not in the **saloon**.

They were not in the **GENERAL STORE**.

They were not at the **BLACKSMITH'S**.

They were not at the *doctor's*.

They were not at the printer's.

And they were not at the *school*. Although that last one didn't surprise me. My cousin Trap never did well in school. His best subject was lunch. Two grilled cheese sandwiches + two cheddar pies = one happy Trap.

Just then I heard someone shouting. It was my cousin. He was at the **RAILROAD STATION**.

Then I heard another voice.

I gulped. It was Mick Muscle Mouse!

The two were arguing. It seemed that both wanted to use the same watering trough for their horses.

Trap's voice was loud and shrill. "You think you're so smart!" he shrieked. "Just wait till my cousin gets here! He'll teach you a thing or two. He's got more brains than a whole library!"

Mick spat on the ground. "Oh, yeah?" he thundered. "Who's your cousin?"

I tried pretending I was a statue. It didn't work. A plump rodent in the crowd spotted me.

"There he is, Mick! The one with the glasses!" he pointed out.

Trap pushed me

forward. I nearly fell flat on my snout.

"Don't push me! I can't stand it when you push me!" I complained.

Mick Muscle Mouse GLARED at me. "You again?" he yelled.

The next thing I knew, I was flying through the air. Mick had just hurled me into the sky. I landed with a loud splash in the watering trough. The horses looked **ANNOYED**.

The **undertaker**, on the other paw, looked thrilled. He jumped up and down and clapped his paws. "Grimsly, let's finish that wooden coffin for the stranger!" he cried. "Something tells me he may need one soon!"

Grimsly snickered and raced away.

Right at that moment, a skinny old lady with a flower in her hat came by. She reminded me of my great-aunt **No Nonsense**. She was one strict rodent.

A coffin the perfect size for Geronimo!

"Mick Muscle Mouse!" I heard the old lady yell. "What are you **doing**?"

Mick looked at the ground. "N-n-nothing, *Teacher*," he stuttered.

She waved her cane in the air. "Very good, Mick," she squeaked. "Because I'm keeping my eye on you. And you'd better b☺h☺v☺! Just because you're not in school anymore doesn't mean you can disobey the rules!"

Mick shuffled his paws. "Oh, of course, *Miss Firm Fur*," he mumbled.

*Miss Firm Fur
the Teacher*

As soon as she left, Mick looked for me. But as my cousin said, I'm one smart mouse. I had already hightailed it out of there.

NO GUNS FOR GERONIMO STILTON

We returned to the saloon. Our rooms were on the first floor. The beds were full of fleas. The walls were stained and peeling. The floor had mounds of **dust**. And the smell was enough to drive a mouse to drink rat poison!

Fleas

Trap pinched his nose. "Germeister, is that you? You should stay away from those **beans**!" he smirked.

Stains

I sighed. Oh, why did I get stuck with such an OBNOXIOUS cousin? He was so annoying. He was so immature. He was so ... clumsy.

Mounds of Dust

I watched in horror as Trap threw open the shutters, knocking over a huge vase of flowers.

It crashed down onto the street.

"Be CAREEEEEEEEFUL! You could hit somebody!" I shrieked.

I scrambled to the window. **Cheese niblets**! The vase *had* hit somebody. Mick Muscle Mouse stood under the window holding a flower. I could see a huge bump forming on his head.

"You again!" he roared. "Stranger, tonight I'm going to **finish** you off! I'm gonna send you packing! You'll be headed for the great big cheese deli in the sky!"

In a flash, the **undertaker** appeared next to him. "Big cheese deli in the sky?" he squeaked, rubbing his paws together.

I ran down to the **saloon**. I had to straighten things out between Mick and me. After all, I never meant to **upset** anyone.

Unfortunately, Mick was another story. He

loved hurting mice. And he was proud of it.

"Stranger! Tonight there'll be one less rodent in Cactus City! Get ready for a shoot-out!" he yelled.

My teeth began to chatter. "I will certainly n-n-n-not get r-r-r-ready f-f-f-for a shootout," I stammered. "GERONIMO STILTON DOES NOT SHOOT G-G-G-GUNS."

Mick rolled his eyes. "This stranger is a 'fraidy mouse!" he cried.

Everyone in the saloon stared at me. "'FRAIDY MOUSE! 'FRAIDY MOUSE!" they chanted.

Squeaks of laughter filled my ears.

NO GUNS FOR GERONIMO STILTON!

I DID NOT DO IT ON PURPOSE!

Before I could decide what to do next...

1 I slipped on a potato peel.
2 I somersaulted into the air.
3 I accidentally kicked Mick in the snout.
4 I grabbed the chandelier.
5 I swung onto the balcony.
6 I slid down the banister.
7 I accidentally head-butted Mick.
8 I fell back on a loose board.
9 I knocked a watermelon into the air.
10 I watched the watermelon land on Mick's head.
11 "I did not do it on purpose!" I apologized to Mick.

1. I slipped on a potato peel.

2. I somersaulted into the air.

3. I accidentally kicked Mick in the snout.

4. I grabbed the chandelier.

5. I swung onto the balcony.

6. I slid down the banister.

7. I accidentally head-butted Mick.

8. I fell back on a loose board.

9. I knocked a watermelon into the air.

10. I watched the watermelon land on Mick's head.

11. "I did not do it on purpose!"

The crowd in the saloon stared at me with respect. "What a mouse! What a fighter! **WHAT A DAREDEVIL!**"

"But I did not do it on purpose! I am not a fighter! I'm not strong!" I protested.

Miss Firm Fur the teacher felt my **MUSCLES**. "Young mouse, I would not have bet a penny on you. I thought Mick would make Swiss cheese out of you," she commented. "But you are strong."

Miss Dolly batted her eyelashes. "*Oooh, Mr. Geronimo,*" she squeaked in a soft voice. "*You are much stronger than Mr. Muscle Mouse. Much, much stronger!*"

I could tell Mick felt awful. He looked as if he were going to cry.

The **undertaker** shook his head. "Too bad they didn't fight it out," he sighed. "No coffins needed here, I guess."

At that moment the earth trembled.

A cloud of dust rolled into town. A group of gun-toting mice galloped behind it.

Someone in the crowd whispered, "The evil gunmice are coming!"

I looked around me. Everyone looked terrified. The doctor, the blacksmith, the teacher, the banker. Yes, even Mick Muscle Mouse looked afraid.

I Am the Strongest!

The gunmice stopped in the center of town. They were pulling a wagon. Inside the wagon sat an **ENORMOUSE** barrel.

I wondered what was inside it. But there was no time to think about it. I was too busy thinking about the leader of the gunmice.

Wicked Whiskers

He was the scariest rodent I had ever seen! He was dressed all in **black** from his leather pants to his **coal-black** hat. His **black** cowrat boots were **EXTRA POINTY**. They looked like they could spear a rodent with one hard paw-kick. His face seemed to be stuck in a permanent scowl. I shivered. Who was this evil gummouse, and what was he doing in **Cactus City**?

Just then I noticed something shiny pinned to his shirt pocket. Rat-munching rattlesnakes! It was a sheriff's star! How could this **EVIL-LOOKING** gunmouse be a sheriff?

A crowd gathered around him.

"Citizens of Cactus City!" the evil-looking gunmouse shouted. "From now on, you will cheer when I enter town. I want singing. I want dancing. And I want a plate of nachos

Applause!

Enough!

with heaping gobs of cheddar!"

Rodents rushed to obey his orders. One led a chorus of "Long Live the Sheriff!" Another started teaching a new line dance. A third produced a plate of steaming nachos.

The sheriff shoved some chips into his mouth. "Too hot, you fool!" he hissed.

Everyone stopped cheering. They stopped singing. They stopped dancing.

They were too scared to squeak.

WHO WILL VOLUNTEER?

Then a voice rose up from the crowd. It was the old lady teacher, *Miss Firm Fur*.

"Citizens of **Cactus City**, you should be ashamed of yourselves!" she cried, waving her cane in the air. "This gunmouse is just a big old bully. Who will stand up to him? I need a strong **VOLUNTEER** to step forward."

Suddenly, someone pushed me from behind.

I should have known. It was my **cousin** Trap.

"Don't push me! I can't stand it when you push me!" I screeched.

Meanwhile, the teacher watched me with an approving eye. "Well done, stranger! I knew you were COURAGEOUS. You are strong! Yes, you are very strong!" she said.

The crowd repeated, "The stranger is strong! He is very strong!"

I TURNED PALE. "But I am not strong, and I am not COURAGEOUS, either," I tried to explain.

No one was listening.

Go, cousin!

"Come on, 'fraidy mouse, don't embarrass the Stilton family!" Thea ordered.

I felt faint. I thought family was supposed to stick by you. But my family was trying to get me killed!

The gunmouse approached me. He took off his sunglasses and stuck his face close to mine. His EYES were as GREEN as a KILLER COBRA'S.

My head began to pound. Oh, how did I get myself into such a mess?

"What's your name, stranger?" the gunmouse asked.

I told him. It wasn't easy. My teeth were chattering so hard, I felt like I was squeaking another language.

"My name is WICKED WHISKERS," the gunmouse snarled. "And I'm going to

make you sorry you ever came to Cactus City!"

I gulped. I was already sorry. I was so sorry, I wanted to break into sobs like a baby mouselet. But how could I? The citizens of Cactus City were counting on me.

"I challenge you to a RODEO match at my ranch. Whoever can ride and tame Bessie wins!" the gunmouse declared. "If you win, I'll leave Cactus City forever."

I looked around me. The rodents of Cactus City were staring at me, worried. I was their last hope. I had no choice.

I accepted the challenge. After all, I told myself, how bad could an animal named Bessie be?

TOGETHER WE CAN DO ANYTHING!

Wicked Whiskers held his paw in the air. The **evil gunmice** jumped back onto their horses. "See you at the **RANCH**!" Wicked sneered at me. Then he left at a gallop.

I was **scared**. I didn't know anything about **RODEOS**. I am a city mouse. The last time I rode a horse was on the mousey-go-round at the Blue Cheese County Carnival. I was dizzy for a week afterward.

I hung my head.

Just then, someone tapped my shoulder. It was Mick Muscle Mouse. "Don't worry, stranger. I'll help you," he said. "Your courage is contagious!"

All the citizens of **Cactus City** clapped.

"Your courage is contagious!" they cheered.

I *smiled*. I didn't tell anyone I really was a 'fraidy mouse. I needed all the help I could get.

"Don't forget us, Gerry Berry!" Thea called. Trap and Benjamin nodded.

"Together we can do anything!" they **shouted**.

I was feeling a lot **better**. I was happy my family was behind me. They really can be great when they want to be. Now if I could just get my sister to stop calling me Gerry Berry....

Your courage is contagious!

HOW THE WEST WAS WON

In 1776, the original thirteen English colonies of North America declared their independence and formed the United States of America. From that moment began the expansion toward the western territories, which were inhabited by Native Americans.

In 1842, the first official trail crossing the Native American territories was established. It was called the Oregon Trail.

In 1862, the U.S. government encouraged settling in the west by enacting a law called the Homestead Act. The Homestead Act provided 160 acres of land to anyone who

wanted to farm, build a house, and live out West for at least five years. Thousands of people migrated to the western territories.

Who were these pioneers who decided to go and conquer the Wild West? They were people of every age, from every walk of life. Whole families left their homes in the East in search of a new life and land to settle.

To cross the Great Plains and the Rocky Mountains, the pioneers traveled for months and months on wagons pulled by oxen, mules, or horses. The trip for these courageous people was hard, but their hearts were filled with enthusiasm and hope....

WICKED WHISKERS'S WATER DAM

Before I went to the evil gunmouse's ranch, I needed to know more about him. Mick told me the whole sad story.

It seemed WICKED WHISKERS was the owner of a piece of land north of Cactus City. A RIVER ran through the land. For years, the river ran straight to Cactus City and was used for farming, cattle, and the citizens of the town. Then Wicked decided he wanted to control Cactus City. He built a dam so the water no longer reached the city. Fields got dry. Cattle got thirsty.

"Now we have to pay Wicked to deliver water to us," Mick explained with a sigh. "He makes us pay for the water in gold."

I was **disgusted**. What kind of mouse would steal water from needy rodents? It was sneaky. It was cruel. It was enough to make me ready to *take on* Wicked Whiskers.

Mick showed me a **MAP**. "We'll need *three days* and *three nights* to reach the Big W, Wicked Whiskers's ranch," he said.

Thea, Trap, and Benjamin were excited.

"This is going to be fabumouse!" Thea cheered.

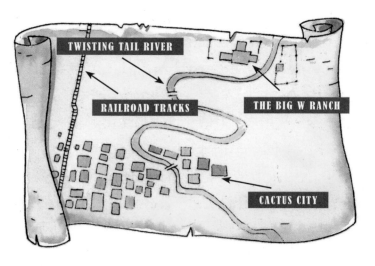

"We'll be like real cowrats!" Trap grinned.

"I love horses!" Benjamin squeaked.

I felt limp. I couldn't ride a horse for three days. I didn't even know how.

Before I could protest, Mick threw me on a horse. It took off at a **gallop**.

I hung on for dear life. One minute, I was hanging upside down from the saddle. The next minute, I was facing the horse's tail.

The crowd watched me go.

"Look at the stranger! He's a regular gymnast!" I heard one mouse cry.

"I've never seen anything like it!" another added.

"He's better than a circus acrobat!" someone else squeaked.

I tried not to sob hysterically. I didn't want to upset the good rodents of **Cactus City**.

STREAMS, SNAKES, AND SCORPIONS

We galloped for hours and hours under the 𝒮𝓊𝓃.

We passed by the **GRAND CANYON**. I stopped at the edge and looked below. Have you ever been to the Grand Canyon? It is unbelievable! I had always thought

> **The GRAND CANYON is located in Arizona. It is a series of gorges carved by the Colorado River flowing through it for thousands and thousands of years. It is 6,000 feet deep, 220 miles long, and from 3 to 18 miles wide.**

the canyon was formed by **VERY HIGH** mountains, but it is not.

It grew **COLD** as night fell. I couldn't stop shivering.

HERE'S WHAT HAPPENED TO ME...

My teeth started chattering...

my tail started aching...

I stubbed my paw on a rock...

I couldn't light the fire...

I fell in a stream...

I ate too many beans...

my stomach got upset...

a snake almost bit me...

I sat on a cactus...

a scorpion attacked me!

Cheese niblets!

We decided to *rest*.

We finally sat around the . Trap played on the banjo. Mick played the harmonica. Then we all sang "Oh! Susannah." I have to admit, it was a *lot of fun*!

BLACK BEAN SOUP

INGREDIENTS:

- I POUND OF DRY BLACK BEANS
- 2 STALKS OF CELERY, CHOPPED
- 2 GARLIC CLOVES, CHOPPED
- I ONION, CHOPPED
- I TEASPOON BLACK PEPPERCORNS

- I BOUILLON CUBE FOR BROTH
- 7 OUNCES CRUSHED TOMATOES
- MIXED DRIED SPICES (CUMIN, HOT PEPPERS, CORIANDER TO TASTE)
- SALT (TO TASTE)

DIRECTIONS:

1. Wash the beans under running water and put them in a large soup pot. Cover them with cold water, and then ask an adult to put them on the stove and turn on the heat.

2. When the water begins to boil, cook the beans for 2 minutes, turn off the heat, and let the beans rest for 1 hour in their liquid. (Do not stir the beans.)

3. Ask an adult to turn on the heat again and add the chopped celery, garlic, onion, and dried spices (to taste) to the pot. Add the teaspoon of peppercorns and the bouillon cube for the soup.

4. Simmer for about 3 hours. Then add the chopped tomatoes and salt to taste.

5. (Optional) Ask an adult to puree one third of the beans in a blender, return them to the pot, and reheat the mixture. This will make the soup thicker.

OH, SUSANNAH:

I come from Alabama
With my banjo on my knee,
I'm going to Louisiana,
My true love for to see.
It rained all night
The day I left,
The weather it was dry,
The sun so hot,
I froze to death,
Susannah, don't you cry.
Oh! Susannah,
Don't you cry for me
For I come from Alabama
With my banjo on my knee.

A REAL COWRAT

That night I fell asleep next to my friends. I was wrapped in a WARM blanket with my head resting on my saddle. Before I drifted off, I gazed up into the sky. Thousands and thousands of STARS kept watch over me.

It was an amazing sight.

In the morning, I nibbled on a tasty breakfast — a stack of yummy cheddar pancakes, bacon, an egg, and two slices of American cheese toast. It was whisker-licking good!

I was feeling great. I always do when my belly is full of cheese. Plus, I was getting used to being on a horse. Mick taught me how to use a lasso. He explained why a horse needs shoes, when to brush it, and how to **FEED** it.

I galloped across the plains with the wind whipping through my whiskers. **Cheesecake**, I was having fun!

The wind whipped through my

I felt like a real **COWRAT**.

Yes, I, Geronimo "Scaredy Mouse" Stilton, was beginning to really like the **WILD, WILD WEST!**

whiskers...I was having fun!

EVERYTHING ON HORSES!

Most horses today live in stables and are used to a tame way of living. It is their nature to live in freedom, but most would find it difficult to readjust to the wild life of the old West.

Horses live in stalls spacious enough to allow them to move and to rest. The stalls are dry and well ventilated, and the floor should be covered with straw for the horses to rest on.

Horses need to eat several meals a day. Their food should be placed inside their stalls, near their water. Besides hay and fresh grass, a horse's diet consists of oats, apples, and carrots.

Horses are very clean animals. They like to be curried (brushed) once a day. This is good for their coats because it removes loose hair and dirt.

A horse gets new shoes every thirty-five to forty days. A horse's hooves are thick but need to be protected by metal shoes. A person who shoes horses is called a blacksmith or a farrier. The farrier removes the old shoes, then cuts and files the hooves and attaches a new pair of shoes.

A NIGHTMARE NAMED . . . BESSIE!

We finally arrived at Wicked Whiskers's ranch. It was dark and spooky-looking. The whole place made **MY FUR CRAWL**.

Just then Wicked sauntered up. "Are you ready to lose, stranger? Are you ready to face **Bessie**?" he cackled.

I tried to look **tough**, but inside I felt like a bowl of cream cheese and jelly.

"N-n-no p-p-p-problem," I stammered. I closed my eyes and took a deep breath. How bad could an animal named Bessie be?

Then I saw him. **Bessie**, I mean. He was an **iMMense** black beast the size of two double-decker cheese delivery trucks. He had **terrifying** red eyes that looked

like they were on fire. His horns were as **LONG** as my tail.

My eyes nearly popped out of my fur. No, Bessie wasn't dangerous. He was deadly!

"W-w-what is that?" I croaked.

Trap snorted. "Wake up and smell the cheese, Germeister," he scoffed. "It's a **bull**, of course. Look at those horns! One poke and you'll run squeaking for your life!"

I felt faint. No wonder Wicked Whiskers knew he would **win** the challenge. I'd never be able to ride Bessie. Not for all the Cheesy Chews in the world!

"Go, cousin, move your tail!" Trap ordered. Then he *PUSHED* me.

"Don't push me! I can't stand it when you push me!" I grabbed the fence. "I changed my mind. **I CAN'T DO THIS!**" I squeaked.

Thea rolled her eyes. "Oh, don't be such a crybaby mouse," she groaned.

So much for her support, I steamed.

A little paw grabbed mine. "Uncle Geronimo, you can do it. I have faith in you!" little Benjamin whispered.

Of course, that's all it took. How could I let my dear sweet nephew down? I could hear Bessie snorting in his pen. *He's not angry*, I told myself. *He's just got a bad cold.*

With shaky paws, I climbed onto his back.

The door of the pen opened.

Bessie took off like a shot!

"Good-bye, Stiltons! Good-bye, Mick! Good-bye, rodents everywhere!" I sobbed.

Bessie the bull

WHY, WHY, WHY?

I tried to hold on to Bessie, but he was too strong for me. In a flash, he'd thrown me to the ground.

"**Help!**" I squeaked as Bessie tried to trample me. I was able to **GET AWAY**, but he was right **ON MY TAIL**. His **HORNS** hooked my shirt. He tossed me into the air. I bounced off the fence. Then I landed back on Bessie.

Suddenly, I spotted my little nephew Benjamin. He was **WAVING HIS PAW** frantically. What was he trying to tell me?

Benjamin started yelling something. It sounded like **HORN**. Or was that *corn*?

Next, my nephew began pointing at his **EAR**. Did he have an **EARACHE**? I love my

I JUMPED ON THE BULL...

HE THREW ME OFF...

HE ALMOST TRAMPLED ME...

HE CHASED AFTER ME...

HE BUTTED ME WITH HIS HORNS

I FLEW THROUGH THE AIR...

I BOUNCED OFF THE FENCE...

I LANDED BACK ON BESSIE!

HE WAS YELLING *HORN*...

OR WAS IT *CORN*?

HE POINTED AT HIS EAR.

nephew, but I couldn't worry about his ears right now.

Just then I glanced down at Bessie's massive neck. That's when I noticed his ear. A huge cactus thorn was stuck on it. Holey cheese! So that's what my nephew was trying to tell me. The **THORN** was making Bessie hopping mad. As I tumbled off his back, I plucked the thorn from his ear.

Bessie stopped snorting. He stopped kicking. He stopped moving. He *laid* his head on my shoulder. And then he smiled. I patted his head and jumped on his back. I couldn't believe it. I, Geronimo Stilton, had tamed **Bessie**!

Benjamin *ran* toward me.

"You saved my life, nephew!" I squeaked. I pulled him up onto **Bessie's** back. We took a victory lap around the ranch.

The rodents of Cactus City arrived. They CLAPPED and CHEERED us on.

I PLUCKED THE THORN...

I PATTED HIS HEAD...

...WE RODE BESSIE!

STRONG RODENTS KNOW HOW TO FORGIVE!

Meanwhile, Wicked Whiskers was **furious**. He couldn't understand why Bessie wasn't MAD anymore.

"Why didn't you make cream cheese out of the stranger?" he screamed at the bull. "My grandma Wimpy Whiskers is tougher than you!"

Bessie **stamped** his hoof. With a snort, he tossed Wicked Whiskers into the air.

The gunmouse fell to the ground. The bull put his hoof on Whiskers's tummy.

Wicked Whiskers's teeth were **CHATTERING**. His tail was twitching. "D-d-d-don't hurt m-m-m-me!"

the gunmouse stammered.

I knelt down next to Wicked Whiskers. The crowd gathered around.

"I think you owe the citizens of Cactus City an **apology**," I said. "You need to give them back their water. You need to stop being a bully."

The gunmouse nodded his head.

"You are right, stranger," he whispered. "I'm sorry for what I've done."

But the crowd wasn't convinced.

"**Let's make him pay for it!**" a mouse screeched.

"Let's get even!" another shouted.

I knew I had to do something quick. "Violence is not the answer," I told the

citizens of **Cactus City**. "Strong rodents know how to forgive. You need to show Wicked Whiskers you are stronger than he is. *You need to let him go.*"

The crowd stopped yelling. They looked embarrassed.

I patted the bull's head. Then I told him to take his hoof off Wicked Whiskers. He did.

Wicked let out a sigh of relief. "Thanks, stranger," he grinned. "You really are a **strong** cowrat!"

He took off his sheriff's *star*. Then he jumped on his horse. His gunmice followed. They galloped off, leaving behind a cloud of **dust**.

YIPPEE!

After the gunmice left, we went to the Twisting Tail River. We found the dam that kept the water from reaching **Cactus City**. It had a handle that locked.

"Geronimo, you unlock that thing," Thea ordered. "Then, Mick, you pull it out. OK, let's go! Go! Go!"

Minutes later, the dam was open. Water flowed out with a loud **WHOOSH**.

"Yippee!" we shouted.

Thea and Trap did a dance. Benjamin clapped his paws. And Mick let out a happy whistle.

As for me, I pulled out a tin cup from my supplies. I knelt down and scooped up some water from the river. I don't know about everyone else, but I was dying of *thirst*!

A Tin Star in Search of a Sheriff

Back in Cactus City, the judge held a meeting.

"This tin star is in search of a sheriff," he announced. "We need a **STRONG** cowrat to defend our *rights*."

The rodents of Cactus City nodded.

Just then a *schoolmouse* ran over to me.

"The stranger is a strong cowrat," he said.

"HE COULD BE OUR NEW SHERIFF."

He placed the tin star in my paw.

I thanked him. I was **HONORED**. But I knew that I couldn't stay in Cactus City After all, I had a newspaper to run back home. And what about my subscription to the Cheese-of-the-Month Club? I couldn't let all that good food go to **waste**.

"Why don't you choose our new sheriff," the judge suggested.

I looked around at the crowd. Everyone was quiet. They were waiting. Waiting for me to make a decision. My head started **POUNDING**. I hate being put on the spot. What if I

made a mistake? What if everyone laughed at me? What if I had permanent hat head when I left **Cactus City**? But that was another story. There wasn't time to worry about it now.

At that moment, I spotted Mick Muscle Mouse. I grinned. Mick was the perfect mouse for the job. He was strong. He was brave. He knew right from wrong.

YOU ARE THE PERFECT SHERIFF!

I **THREW** the **star** to Mick. He caught it in midair.

"You are the perfect **SHERiFF** for this city, friend," I said.

Tears **SPRANG** to Mick's eyes. Anyone could see he was a big mouse with **A BIG HEART**. "I'll do my best to earn your **RESPECT**," Mick said to the crowd.

Everyone cheered.

I'LL DO MY BEST!

Suddenly, a swirling cloud of **dust** enveloped me. My head started spinning. My heart started racing. What was happening? I felt like I was flying, but I wasn't sitting in a cozy seat watching a movie. I wasn't even on an airplane!

I LET OUT A SCREAM...

Where Am I?

I woke up startled.

"Where am I?" I mumbled.

I looked around.

I was in my room.

In my home.

In New Mouse City!

No, I was not in the Wild West after all. It was only a **dream**.

I heard a droning sound.

The TV was **ON**.

Then I remembered something. I had been watching television before I fell asleep. I was watching an adventure story about the **WILD, WILD WEST!**

"OH! SUSANNAH"

I looked for a pail...

I shuffled to the bathroom. I looked for a pail so I could **wash** my face.

Then I remembered...I wasn't in the Wild West.

I went down to the kitchen for breakfast. I looked for a can of beans to eat.

Then I remembered...I wasn't in the Wild West.

I looked for beans...

I went outside. I looked for my horse to ride to **work**.

Then I remembered...I

wasn't in the Wild West anymore.

At last I realized what was happening.

I WAS MISSING THE WILD WEST. I wanted to go back — for real.

I took a taxi to the office. I hummed "Oh! Susannah" as we zoomed along. It seemed as if there were a thousand cars on the street. Rodents beeped. Brakes screeched. What a rat race! I needed a break.

That's when I got an idea. No, not just any idea. A great, perfect, fabumouse idea!

I raced up the stairs of *The Rodent's Gazette*. I called Thea, Trap, and Benjamin into my office.

"I feel like taking a *TRIP*," I announced. "Who wants to go with me

I looked for my horse...

to the **WILD, WILD WEST**?"

Of course, everyone wanted to go. My family loves to travel. And they love adventure.

Trap pushed me toward the door. "Good for you, Germeister!" he chuckled. "It's about time you stopped being a scaredy mouse. You're gonna love the **WILD, WILD WEST**!"

I rolled my eyes. But then I smiled. I had to admit; for once, I knew my cousin was right.

Now if I could just get him to stop calling me Germeister...

Let's go to the Wild, Wild West!

THE ABC'S OF
THE WILD WEST

BRIDLE: a horse's headgear, which carries the bit and reins that the rider uses to guide the horse.

BUNKHOUSE: a very simple wooden building where the ranch hands slept.

CANTER: a horse's three-beat gait that resembles a gallop but is smoother and slower.

CORRAL: an enclosure or pen where livestock is kept. Corral is also what the settlers called the circle of wagons formed by wagon trains when they stopped to rest during a long trip.

COWBOY: a cattle ranch hand who tends the livestock from horseback. Cowboys were experts in driving a herd along trails that stretched for miles among the western United States.

GAIT: the sequence of footsteps a horse takes when it moves forward, such as a canter, gallop, trot, rack, pace, or walk.

GALLOP: a horse's fast three-beat gait. When your horse gallops, it seems as if you're flying!

LASSO: a rope or long thong of leather with a slip noose, used to catch horses and cattle. Roping is one of the many skills that cowboys needed in their work.

LIVESTOCK TRAILS: paths cowboys used when driving herds of livestock to market. These trails were many miles long, and a cattle drive could take several weeks to complete.

MUSTANG: a wild horse of the western plains. It is small and hardy, a descendant of horses brought to North America by the Spaniards.

RANCH: a large farm for raising horses, cattle, or sheep.

REINS: the straps used by a rider to guide a horse. The reins are fastened to a bit in the horse's mouth.

RODEO: a public contest among cowboys showing the skills they use in their work, such as riding bucking broncos and bulls, roping calves, and wrestling steers to the ground.

SADDLE: a padded and usually leather-covered seat for a horseback rider. The saddle is kept in place by straps that go around the horse's belly.

SALOON: a typical gathering place in the Wild West where people ate, played cards, listened to music, and danced.

SHERIFF: a law officer whose main jobs are to keep order and make sure no laws are being broken.

SPURS: pointed metal pieces attached to a horseback rider's boot heels. A cowboy would urge his horse by pressing the spurs into the horse's side.

STAGECOACH: a carriage, usually drawn by a six-horse team, that transported passengers and mail in the old West.

TAME: to train a wild animal so that it gets used to being around humans.

THOROUGHBRED: a valuable horse whose ancestors are English mares and Arabian stallions. Thoroughbreds are light and fast, so they are used especially for racing.

TROT: a horse's medium-fast two-beat gait. The horse moves its feet in diagonal pairs—just as humans swing their arms as they walk.

Geronimo's Joke Contest Winners!

Special thanks to all my mouse friends who sent me jokes! All the jokes were absolutely hilari-mouse. In fact, I laughed so hard, I almost broke my funny bone! Here are some of my favorites.

If a mouse lost his tail, where would he go to get a new one?
A re-tail store!

From Flannery in Washington State

When should a mouse carry an umbrella?
When it's raining cats and dogs!

From Caleb in Maryland

What animal is a tattletale?
A pig. It always squeals on you!

From Emily in Ohio

What's a mouse's favorite state?
Swissconsin!

Why do rodents like earthquakes?
Because they like to shake, rattle, and MOLE.

From Amanda in California

What's the tallest building in the world?
The library, of course! It has the most stories.

What do you call something easy to chew?
A ch-easy chew!
From Darianne in New Hampshire

What martial art does Geronimo Stilton like to practice?
Tai Cheese!
From Ryan in Texas

What happens to a cat when it eats a lemon?
It turns into a sourpuss!
From Tiffany in Florida

How do you make a tissue dance?
You put a little boogie in it.
From Zachery in New Jersey

What do you call a group of mice in disguise?
A mouse-querade party!
From the Freed family in Michigan

How does a mouse feel after a shower?
Squeaky clean!
From Ian in Washington State

What do you call a mouse that's the size of an elephant?
Enor-mouse!
From Parker

Who was the first cat to come to America?
Christo-fur Colum-puss!
From Nora in Virginia

What's black and white and red all over?
The Rodent's Gazette! It's READ all over.

ABOUT THE AUTHOR

Born in New Mouse City, Mouse Island, Geronimo Stilton is Rattus Emeritus of Mousomorphic Literature and of Neo-Ratonic Comparative Philosophy. For the past twenty years, he has been running *The Rodent's Gazette*, New Mouse City's most widely read daily newspaper.

Stilton was awarded the Ratitzer Prize for his scoop on *The Curse of the Cheese Pyramid.* He has also received the Andersen 2000 Prize for Personality of the Year. One of his best-sellers won the 2002 eBook Award for world's best ratlings' electronic book. His works have been published all over the globe.

In his spare time, Mr. Stilton collects antique cheese rinds and plays golf. But what he most enjoys is telling stories to his nephew Benjamin.

The Rodent's Gazette

1. Main Entrance
2. Printing presses (where the books and newspaper are printed)
3. Accounts department
4. Editorial room (where the editors, illustrators, and designers work)
5. Geronimo Stilton's office
6. Storage space for Geronimo's books

Don't miss any of my other fabumouse adventures!

#1 Lost Treasure of the Emerald Eye

#2 The Curse of the Cheese Pyramid

#3 Cat and Mouse in a Haunted House

#4 I'm Too Fond of My Fur!

#5 Four Mice Deep in the Jungle

#6 Paws Off, Cheddarface!

#7 Red Pizzas for a Blue Count

#8 Attack of the Bandit Cats

#9 A Fabumouse Vacation for Geronimo

#10 All Because of a Cup of Coffee

#11 It's Halloween, You Fraidy Mouse!

#12 Merry Christmas, Geronimo!

#13 The Phantom of the Subway

#14 The Temple of the Ruby of Fire

#15 The Mona Mousa Code

#16 A Cheese-Colored Camper

#17 Watch Your Whiskers, Stilton

#18 Shipwreck on the Pirate Islands

#19 My Name is Stilton, Geronimo Stilton

#20 Surf's Up, Geronimo

and coming soon

#22 The Secret of Cacklefur Castle

Map of New Mouse City

1. Industrial Zone
2. Cheese Factories
3. Angorat International Airport
4. WRAT Radio and Television Station
5. Cheese Market
6. Fish Market
7. Town Hall
8. Snotnose Castle
9. The Seven Hills of Mouse Island
10. Mouse Central Station
11. Trade Center
12. Movie Theater
13. Gym
14. Catnegie Hall
15. Singing Stone Plaza
16. The Gouda Theater
17. Grand Hotel
18. Mouse General Hospital
19. Botanical Gardens
20. Cheap Junk for Less (Trap's store)
21. Parking Lot
22. Mouseum of Modern Art
23. University and Library
24. *The Daily Rat*
25. *The Rodent's Gazette*
26. Trap's House
27. Fashion District
28. The Mouse House Restaurant
29. Environmental Protection Center
30. Harbor Office
31. Mousidon Square Garden
32. Golf Course
33. Swimming Pool
34. Blushing Meadow Tennis Courts
35. Curlyfur Island Amusement Park
36. Geronimo's House
37. New Mouse City Historic District
38. Public Library
39. Shipyard
40. Thea's House
41. New Mouse Harbor
42. Luna Lighthouse
43. The Statue of Liberty

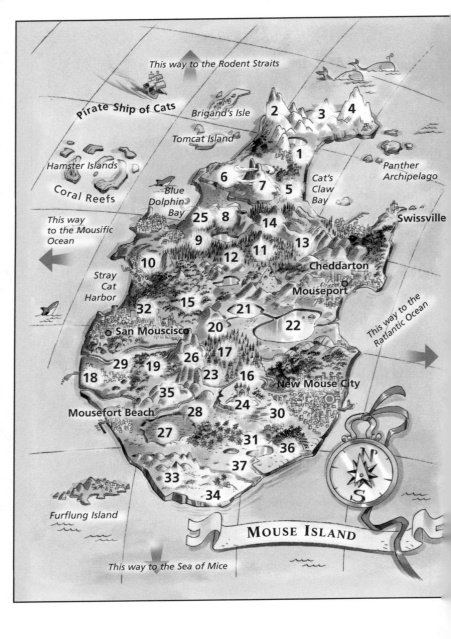

This way to the Rodent Straits

Pirate Ship of Cats

Brigand's Isle

Tomcat Island

Hamster Islands

Coral Reefs

Blue
Dolphin
Bay

This way
to the Mousific
Ocean

Stray
Cat
Harbor

San Mouscisco

Mousefort Beach

Furflung Island

This way to the Sea of Mice

Cat's
Claw
Bay

Panther
Archipelago

Swissville

Cheddarton

Mouseport

New Mouse City

This way to the
Ratlantic Ocean

MOUSE ISLAND

1 2 3 4 5 6 7 8 9 10 11 12 13 14 15 16 17 18 19 20 21 22 23 24 25 26 27 28 29 30 31 32 33 34 35 36 37

Map of Mouse Island

1. Big Ice Lake
2. Frozen Fur Peak
3. Slipperyslopes Glacier
4. Coldcreeps Peak
5. Ratzikistan
6. Transratania
7. Mount Vamp
8. Roastedrat Volcano
9. Brimstone Lake
10. Poopedcat Pass
11. Stinko Peak
12. Dark Forest
13. Vain Vampires Valley
14. Goose Bumps Gorge
15. The Shadow Line Pass
16. Penny Pincher Lodge
17. Nature Reserve Park
18. Las Ratayas Marinas
19. Fossil Forest
20. Lake Lake
21. Lake Lake Lake
22. Lake Lakelakelake
23. Cheddar Crag
24. Cannycat Castle
25. Valley of the Giant Sequoia
26. Cheddar Springs
27. Sulfurous Swamp
28. Old Reliable Geyser
29. Vole Vale
30. Ravingrat Ravine
31. Gnat Marshes
32. Munster Highlands
33. Mousehara Desert
34. Oasis of the Sweaty Camel
35. Cabbagehead Hill
36. Rattytrap Jungle
37. Rio Mosquito

Dear mouse friends,
Thanks for reading, and farewell
till the next book.
It'll be another whisker-licking-good
adventure, and that's a promise!

Geronimo Stilton